For Marnie, with love

GLOSSARY

AHOY! – a shout used as a greeting or to call attention

MAINSAIL – the lowest and largest sail on the main mast

POOP DECK – the highest deck, which often forms the roof of a cabin in the stern, or rear, of a ship

BURGEE – the flag used to identify a ship

ANCHORS AWEIGH! – a call to let sailors know that the anchor is being hauled up from the seabed so the ship is free to sail

ROGUE WAVE – an enormous, unpredictable wave

BATTEN THE HATCHES – prepare for a storm by closing doors and portholes

FURL – roll up tightly

JIB – a triangular sail at the front of a ship

DOLDRUMS – an often windless area near the equator where sailing ships can get stuck; also an exasperating period of time when nothing happens

TURNBUCKLE – a connecting screw used to keep ropes taut

MIZZENMAST – a shorter mast behind the main mast

DISTRESS SIGNAL – a signal sent from a ship in trouble

Copyright © 2024 by Sophie Blackall
All rights reserved. Published in the United States
by Anne Schwartz Books, an imprint of Random House Children's
Books, a division of Penguin Random House LLC, New York.
Anne Schwartz Books and the colophon are trademarks of Penguin
Random House LLC.
Visit us on the Web! rhcbooks.com
Educators and librarians, for a variety of teaching tools,
visit us at RHTeachersLibrarians.com

Library of Congress Cataloging-in-Publication Data
is available upon request.
ISBN 978-0-593-42939-6 (trade) —
ISBN 978-0-593-42940-2 (lib. bdg.) —
ISBN 978-0-593-42941-9 (ebook)

The text of this book is hand-lettered by the artist.
The illustrations in this book were drawn in Procreate with a digital
6B pencil, digital brushes, gouache, and watercolor.
Book design by Martha Rago

MANUFACTURED IN CHINA
10 9 8 7 6 5 4 3 2 1   First Edition

AHOY!

SOPHIE BLACKALL

a·s·
anne schwartz books

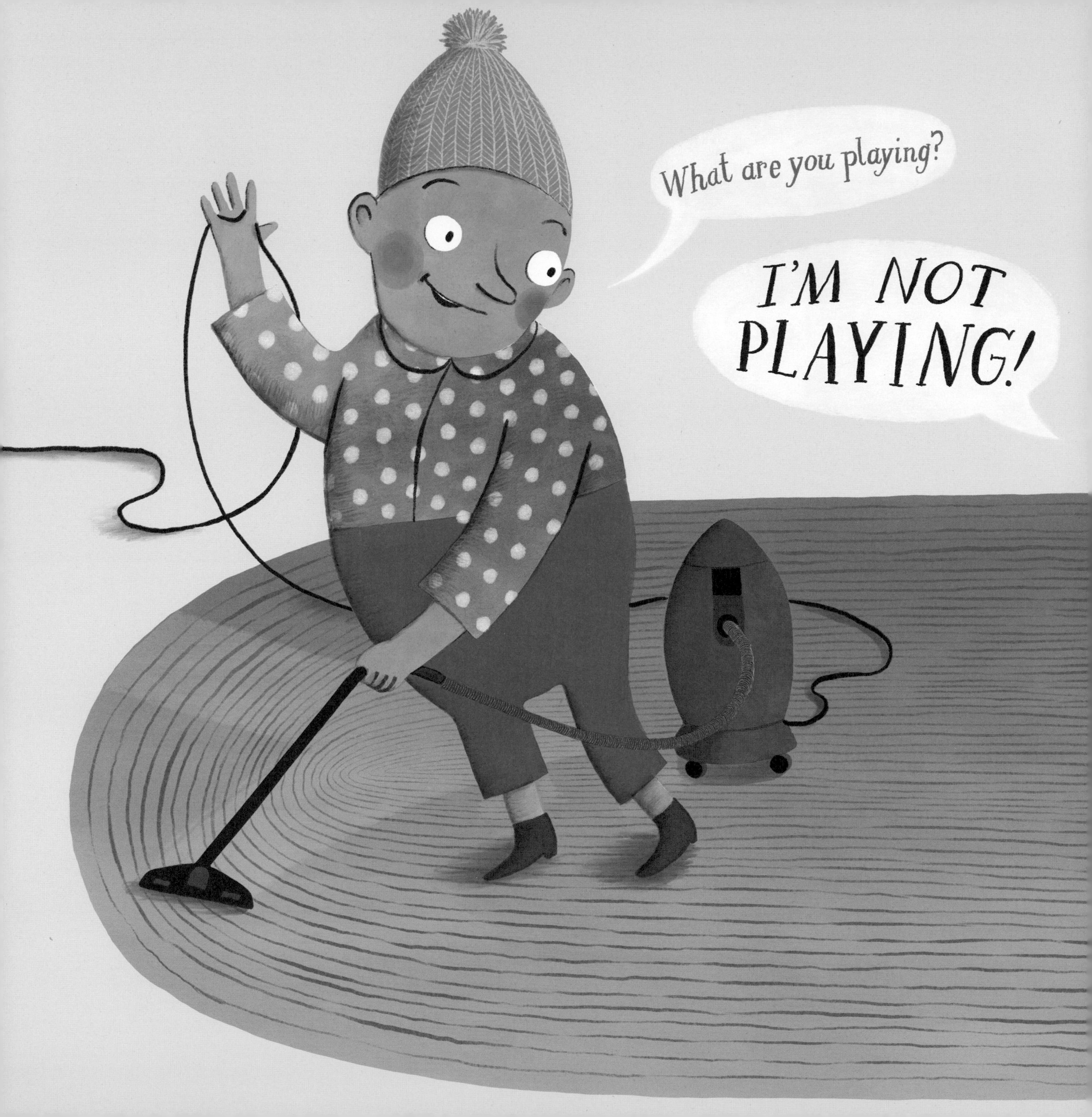
What are you playing?
I'M NOT PLAYING!

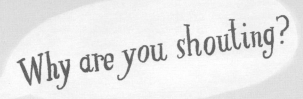

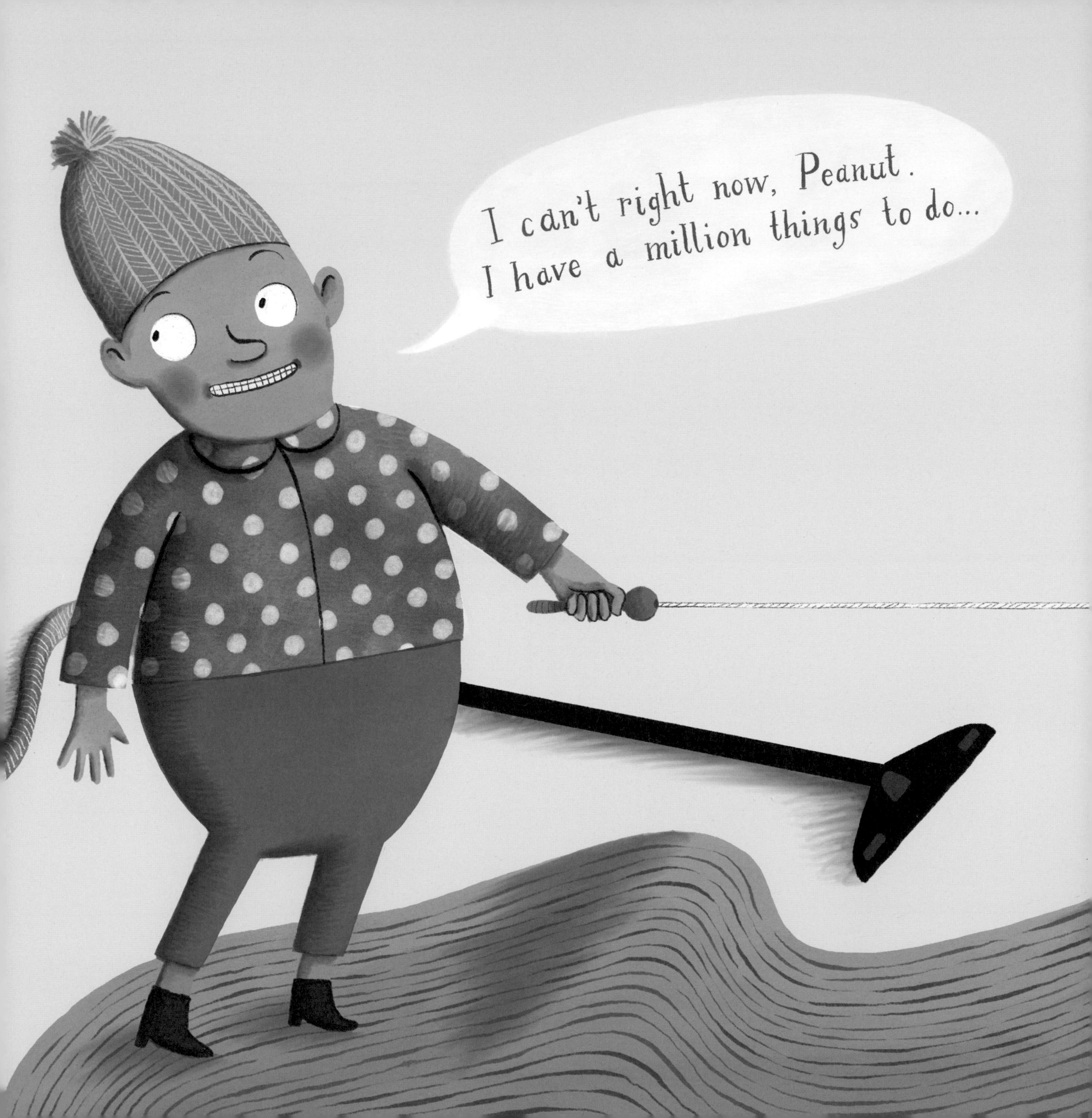
I can't right now, Peanut.
I have a million things to do...

IF WE DON'T LEAVE SOON, WE'LL BE EATEN BY SHARKS! ALSO, YOU NEED TO DRAW THE MAP!
You'll let me help with the map?

HOIST THE BURGEE!

ANCHORS...

LOOK OUT! ROGUE WAVE!
ALL HANDS ON DECK! BATTEN THE HATCHES! FURL THE JIB!

Not a moment too soon!